Minnesota

Wisconsin

Michigan

Maine

Vermont

New Hampshire

Massachusetts

New York

Rhode Island

Connecticut

Pennsylvania

New Jersey

Iowa

Illinois

Ohio

Indiana

Delaware

Maryland

West Virginia

Virginia

Washington, D.C.

Kansas

MISSOURI

Kentucky

North Carolina

Oklahoma

Tennessee

South Carolina

Arkansas

Alabama

Georgia

Mississippi

Louisiana

Florida

N

W

E

S

The Twelve Days of Christmas in Missouri

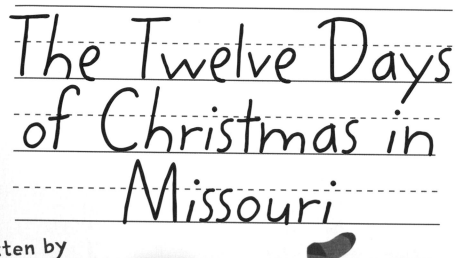

written by
Ann Ingalls

illustrated by
Laura Huliska-Beith

STERLING CHILDREN'S BOOKS
New York

Hey, Cody!

I'm so glad you're coming to Missouri for the holidays! People here say, "I'm from Missouri. You've got to show me." Well, I am going to show you just what a great state Missouri is. We're going to travel this state up, down, backward, forward, and sideways.

Bring your binoculars, snow boots, and warm woolies. We'll count bald eagles at Squaw Creek National Wildlife Refuge and go spelunking, or exploring in caves. Missouri has over 6,000! And guess what we'll see in those caves? Bats! Millions of them! But don't worry—most of them will be hibernating when we get there.

By the end of the week, you'll have seen two of the most important rivers in the United States: the muddy Missouri and the mighty Mississippi. And I'll be giving you gifts along the way— one for each of the Twelve Days of Christmas. See you soon!

Your cousin,
Laila

P. S. Dad said it just wouldn't be right if we didn't celebrate your visit with ice cream cones. After all, they're Missouri's official dessert: Ice cream cones were a big hit at the 1904 World's Fair in St. Louis.

Dear Mom and Dad,

As soon as I got off the plane, Aunt Kathy, Uncle Brad, and Laila met me at the gate with a big sign that read, "Welcome, Cody!" Laila handed me a small dogwood tree with a tiny little bluebird perched on top. I named him Bitsy!

After that, we got in the car and drove straight to the Loess Bluffs National Wildlife Refuge in Mound City. There were thousands of snow geese and ducks, and hundreds of bald eagles. (No, I didn't count every one.)

The birds fly out at dawn to feed and come back about ten in the morning to roost. They fly out again around four o'clock in the afternoon and return when the sun sets. They beeped, squeaked, and squawked like a bunch of chickens. On our way home, Laila told me this riddle:

Q: How do you catch a unique bird?
A: Unique up on it.

Q: How do you catch a tame bird?
A: The tame way, unique up on it!

I am having such a good time already. I can't wait to see what they have planned for tomorrow!

Your bird-watching son,

Cody

WELCOME TO MISSOURI!
THE SHOW-ME STATE

On the first day of Christmas,
my cousin gave to me . . .

a bluebird in
a dogwood tree.

Welcome, Cody!

VISIT THE KANSAS CITY ZOO

Dear Mom and Dad,

Bright and early this morning, we drove to the Pony Express Museum in St. Joseph, Missouri. There we learned that three men, William Hepburn Russell, Alexander Majors, and William Bradford Waddell, had an idea to begin a mail delivery system that would stretch from Missouri to California.

It started on April 3, 1860, when a rider left on horseback from the Pike's Peak Stables. He carried saddlebags called mochilas that held about 20 pounds of mail.

One hundred and eighty-three riders delivered the mail from one post to the next. They rode day and night across plains, deserts, and mountains in all kinds of crazy weather. The journey from Missouri to California usually took eight or nine days. Most of the riders were men, but some women signed up to ride too. One of the youngest riders, Bronco Charlie Miller, was only eleven. Robert Haslam, or Pony Bob, was a really fast rider— he rode nearly 400 miles in 36 hours.

It makes my bottom sore just to think about it!

After seeing the exhibits, Laila and I tried on pioneer clothing and used a real lasso to rope a wooden horse.

Love,

Cody

Mochila

On the second day of Christmas,
my cousin gave to me . . .

2 brave steeds

Morgan

Thoroughbred

and a bluebird
in a dogwood tree.

Dear Mom and Dad,

Today, after finishing a big stack of pancakes, we drove straight to the Kansas City Zoo. On the way there, Laila said, "What's red and white and swims with the penguins?" I knew what I wanted to say, but I couldn't believe it until I saw it. It was Santa! He was all decked out head to toe in his Santa suit, and he dipped and dove with the penguins. That had to be one of the chilliest pools ever. Before we left the zoo, we watched the cheetahs race around a track and waved hello to the orangutans and gorillas.

For dinner, we filled up on Kansas City-style barbecue: the meat was slow-roasted over a wood fire, then topped off with a thick tomato and molasses sauce. Yummy! There are more than 100 barbecue restaurants around town.

Want to come back in October for the American Royal? Hundreds of folks compete to win prizes for the tastiest meats and side dishes. There are sure to be leftovers!

Your totally stuffed son,

Cody

On the third day of Christmas,
my cousin gave to me . . .

3 diving birds

2 brave steeds, and a
bluebird in a dogwood tree.

Hey Mom and Dad,

Do-si-do and gather round! This is how a square dance sounds:

Couple number one, balance and swing.

Lead out to the right and form a ring.

Leave her be and circle three.

Put her on your right and circle four.

Two little hobos elbow swing.

Everybody home and everybody swing.

Today we went to the Hallsville Community Center for a Missouri fiddle jam session. They played bluegrass music and had a square dance! After watching for a little bit, we got to strum fiddles and learn how to square dance. It wasn't easy, but it sure was fun. Laila and I only ran into each other four or five times!

By the end of the dance we were super dizzy—and super hungry! We sat down to a fine potluck supper. I had Ozark Pudding, President Harry Truman's favorite dessert. (He was from Missouri, did you know?) The lady who made the pudding gave me her recipe. Let's make it when I get home!

Your do-si-do-ing son,
Cody

On the fourth day of Christmas, my cousin gave to me . . .

4 square dancers

3 diving birds,
2 brave steeds,
and a bluebird in
a dogwood tree.

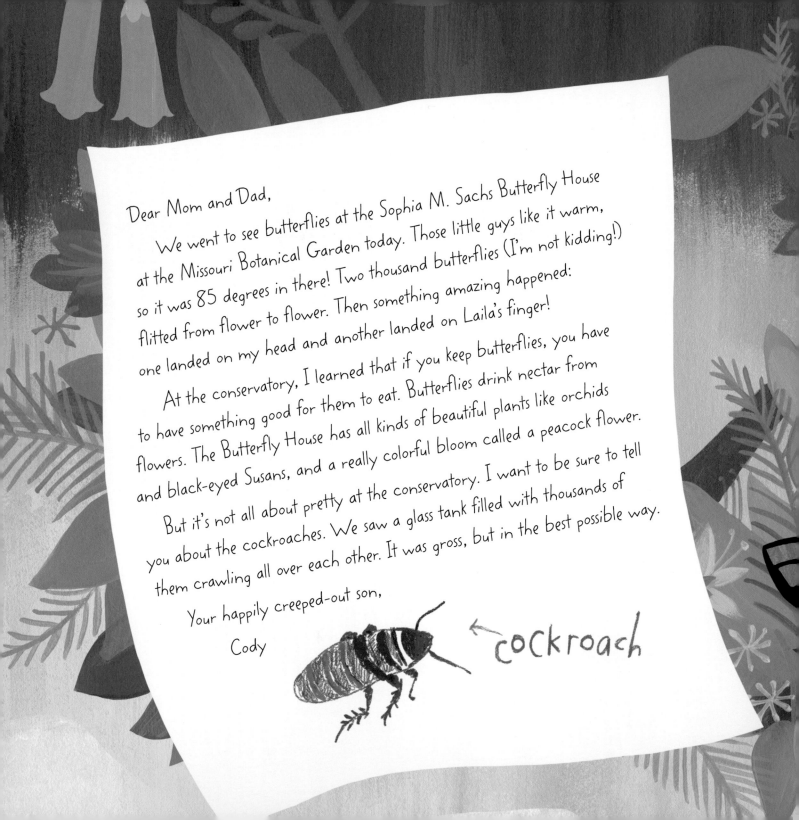

Dear Mom and Dad,

We went to see butterflies at the Sophia M. Sachs Butterfly House at the Missouri Botanical Garden today. Those little guys like it warm, so it was 85 degrees in there! Two thousand butterflies (I'm not kidding!) flitted from flower to flower. Then something amazing happened: one landed on my head and another landed on Laila's finger!

At the conservatory, I learned that if you keep butterflies, you have to have something good for them to eat. Butterflies drink nectar from flowers. The Butterfly House has all kinds of beautiful plants like orchids and black-eyed Susans, and a really colorful bloom called a peacock flower.

But it's not all about pretty at the conservatory. I want to be sure to tell you about the cockroaches. We saw a glass tank filled with thousands of them crawling all over each other. It was gross, but in the best possible way.

Your happily creeped-out son,

Cody

← cockroach

On the fifth day of Christmas,
my cousin gave to me . . .

5 golden birdwings

4 square dancers,
3 diving birds, 2 brave steeds,
and a bluebird in a dogwood tree.

Hi Mom! Hi Dad!

Ever been to a ship-shaped museum? Well, I have. Today we went to the Titanic Museum in Branson. We saw a grand staircase built to look just like the one on the Titanic. The museum also has a deck chair from the actual ship. In the kids area, there are ramps tilted like the decks on the ship did when it sank. Pretty amazing.

After that, Aunt Kathy told us to put on our pajamas, but she didn't say why! When we pulled up to the 1906 depot in downtown Branson to board a special Christmas train, it all made sense. We got to ride in our pj's!

"All aboard!" cried the conductor as we stepped onto the old restored train and found our seats. No sooner had we pulled out of the depot than we were served piping hot mugs of cocoa topped with whipped cream and chocolate sprinkles. The ride was so pretty I couldn't stop looking out the window.

Your hot cocoa-loving son,
Cody

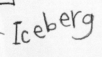
← Iceberg

On the sixth day of Christmas,
my cousin gave to me . . .

6 cups of cocoa

5 golden birdwings,
4 square dancers, 3 diving birds,
2 brave steeds, and a bluebird
in a dogwood tree.

Dear Mom and Dad,

We went back in time today to see what Christmas looked like long ago. At the St. Charles Christmas Traditions Festival, lots of folks were dressed as they would have been in the 1800s. We watched the drum and fife corps march down cobblestone streets and visited with storybook characters. We sipped warm cups of wassail, made from orange and cranberry juices, and apple cider. It is cinnamon-y sweet. As Aunt Kathy said, "It warms the cockles of your heart." Even that sounded old-fashioned! I think it means that it warms you all over, and that's true for sure.

The snow was falling when we hopped aboard a carriage for a ride through town. Hearing the drummers drum, the sleigh bells ring, and the horses' hooves clip-clop, clip-clop was something I don't think I'll ever forget. I wish you'd been there.

Warm to the tips of my toes,
Cody

On the seventh day of Christmas,
my cousin gave to me . . .

7 drummers
drumming
6 cups of cocoa,
5 golden birdwings,
4 square dancers,
3 diving birds, 2 brave steeds,
and a bluebird in a dogwood tree.

Dear Mom and Dad,

We went back to St. Charles today to see Santas from all over the world. Well, you and I know there is only one true Santa, but people from other countries and times imagine him wearing different clothing and carrying different things. We saw Frontier Santa, Père Noël, Father Christmas, Kris Kringle, MacNicholas, Saint Nicholas, and a few more. It was hard to keep them all straight! Jack Frost and the Sugar Plum Fairy were there, too.

We also visited the Lewis and Clark Boat House and Nature Center. Meriwether Lewis and William Clark were sent out by President Thomas Jefferson to find a route to the Pacific and to learn about native plants and animals in the West.

They discovered over 200 plants and animals not known to people who lived in the East. We saw boats built to look just like those that the explorers used and we got to touch some of the animals they found on their trip: a bobcat, a blue heron, a woodchuck, a prairie dog, a squirrel, a goose, and a duck.

As we left the museum, we were given shiny pressed pennies with Lewis and Clark's images. I'm going to keep mine in a safe place.

Your explorer,
Cody

On the eighth day of Christmas,
my cousin gave to me . . .

8 smiling Santas

7 drummers drumming,
6 cups of cocoa,
5 golden birdwings, 4 square dancers,
3 diving birds, 2 brave steeds,
and a bluebird in a dogwood tree.

Dear Mom and Dad,

Wow! We had such a great day today! We went to Fantastic Caverns in Springfield, Missouri, where we rode a tram on a dry path that was once an ancient river. We saw all kinds of crazy formations—some shaped like mushrooms, others like toothy grins or spiky crystal porcupines.

All of them were made by water dripping through limestone and eating away at the rock, one drop at a time. This leaves spaces that grow into caves. Cave formations that hang from the ceiling are called stalactites and those that build up from the floor are called stalagmites.

Here's a riddle to help you remember:

What did the grouchy stalagmite say to the stalactite?

"Quit dripping on me!"

People have never lived in these caverns, but lots of animals have. There are raccoons, possums, foxes, and a shy little fish called the Ozarks cavefish. But Laila and I think the most interesting animals in the cave are the salamanders. They are bright orange with spots and bulgy eyes—and they are so wiggly!

Your spelunking son,

Cody

Stalactite

Stalagmite

On the ninth day of Christmas,
my cousin gave to me . . .

9 salamanders

8 smiling Santas,
7 drummers drumming,
6 cups of cocoa,
5 golden birdwings, 4 square dancers,
3 diving birds, 2 brave steeds,
and a bluebird in a dogwood tree.

Dear Mom and Dad,

What do the world's largest pair of underwear, the world's longest pencil, and a shoelace factory have in common? You can see all of them at the City Museum in St. Louis! Laila and I made a list of everything we wanted to do there, sort of like a scavenger hunt.

In one area of the museum called Monstrocity there are planes and fire trucks and a tower called the Keep. In the Keep I felt like I was in an ancient castle. We climbed steps, structures, bridges, and slides. Then Laila said, "I saved the best for last." We hopped on a slide that was ten stories tall. I screamed my lungs out!

On our way home, we visited the tallest man-made monument in the United States—the Gateway Arch. It is 630 feet tall, but it only took us four minutes to ride up to the top, where we had a really nice view of the Mississippi River. It carries more water than any other river in the United States. Let's come back in the summer and take a riverboat ride on the Mississippi. Sound like fun (hint, hint)?

Your high-riding, slip-sliding son,
Cody

St. Louis Arch →

On the tenth day of Christmas,
my cousin gave to me . . .

10 sliding stories

9 salamanders,
8 smiling Santas,
7 drummers drumming,
6 cups of cocoa,
5 golden birdwings,
4 square dancers,
3 diving birds, **2** brave steeds,
and a bluebird in a dogwood tree.

Hi, Mom! Hi, Dad!

Aunt Kathy and Uncle Brad made me and Laila get up super early this morning, but it was for a good reason. We drove straight to Crown Center in Kansas City to go ice-skating. We slipped and slid but were mostly able to stay up on our skates. I couldn't quite master a figure eight without falling, but Laila did.

When we'd skated our hearts out and it got dark, we went to see the Plaza lights. Holy mackerel! Uncle Brad says they have over 80 miles of lights! Hundreds of thousands of bulbs brighten up the buildings at the Country Club Plaza.

Then Uncle Brad announced, "No trip to the Plaza is complete without a stop at Winstead's for a skyscraper." What in that world is that, you ask? It's 64 ounces of chocolate, vanilla, or strawberry milkshake.

It doesn't exactly touch the sky, but it sure feels like it.

De-LIGHT-fully yours,

Cody

Skyscraper

On the eleventh day of Christmas,
my cousin gave to me . . .
11 skaters skating

10 sliding stories,
9 salamanders,
8 smiling Santas,
7 drummers drumming,
6 cups of cocoa, 5 golden birdwings,
4 square dancers, 3 diving birds, 2 brave steeds,
and a bluebird in a dogwood tree.

Dear Mom and Dad,

Today we had another early morning! We got up at the crack of dawn, packed bags of groceries in the car, and headed to Harvesters, which is a food collection and distribution site. We packed tons of BackSnacks, snacks for school-aged kids. Each BackSnack has enough food for one kid to eat all weekend if there isn't enough at home. I'm so glad we were able to help. I didn't realize there are many families who need it.

In the afternoon we went to the National Museum of Toys and Miniatures. Good golly! They have more than 50,000 toys. There are dollhouses taller than Uncle Brad, filled with itty bitty doll furniture—I've never seen such small tables! Then there are rooms of robots, thousands of normal-size dolls, and the world's only two-story toytisserie, a really cool tower of toys that spins slowly so you can see everything. And they've got a bunch of micro-curiosities—teeny-tiny toys and figures that can only be seen clearly through microscopes. They've even got a flea circus. It's amazing! You've got to see this place. I'm excited to see you both, but I have had a great time here in Missouri! I'll miss Laila, Aunt Kathy, Uncle Brad, and all our adventures when I get home.

Your completely amazed son,
Cody

BACKSNACK

MILK · POWER MIX · BRAN CEREAL · STEW

On the twelfth day of Christmas,
my cousin gave to me . . .

12 tiny tables
11 skaters skating,
10 sliding stories,
9 salamanders,
8 smiling Santas,
7 drummers drumming,
6 cups of cocoa,
5 golden birdwings,
4 square dancers,
3 diving birds,
2 brave steeds,
and a bluebird in a
dogwood tree.

MISSOURI: THE SHOW-ME STATE

St. Louis CARDINALS

AVERAGE TEMPERATURES
JANUARY: 22° to 40°
JULY: 69° to 90°

MISSOURI
THE CAVE STATE
OVER 6,000

YOGI BERRA
IT AIN'T ALL OVER TIL IT'S OVER

MISTY COPELAND
PRIMA BALLERINA

RUDOLPH'S HITA LGT PARADE

INDEPENDENCE MO.
HOME OF HARRY S. TRUMAN

SPORTING
KANSAS CITY
SOCCER TEAM

GARDEN GLOW
MISSOURI BOTANICAL GARDEN

MISSOURI
THE SHOW-ME STATE

Missouri: The Show-Me State

St. Louis Arch

Capital: Jefferson City • **State Abbreviation:** MO • **Largest City:** Kansas City

State Bird: eastern bluebird • **State Tree:** flowering dogwood

State Flower: white hawthorn blossom • **State Insect:** honeybee

State Animal: Missouri mule • **State Stone:** mozarkite

State Reptile: three-toed box turtle • **State Song:** Missouri Waltz

SOME FAMOUS MISSOURIANS:

George Caleb Bingham (1811–1879) was well known for his portraits and paintings of life on the Missouri frontier. Many people believe that Bingham was one of the greatest American-born artists.

George Washington Carver (1864–1943) was a world-famous botanist and inventor who made important agricultural discoveries and inventions. His research on peanuts, sweet potatoes, and other products helped poor southern farmers change their crops and improve their diets.

Samuel Clemens (1835–1910) was born in Florida, Missouri. He moved to the Mississippi River town of Hannibal when he was four. Under the pen name Mark Twain, he wrote *The Adventures of Tom Sawyer* and *Adventures of Huckleberry Finn*, among other novels.

Walt Disney (1901–1966) was a cartoonist and pioneer of animated films. He grew up in Marceline and Kansas City. Disney created the first animated cartoon with sound, *Steamboat Willie*, which introduced the world to Mickey Mouse.

Edwin Powell Hubble (1889–1953) was born in Marshfield and became one of the world's leading astronomers. In 1925, he presented the first system for classifying galaxies. His work showed that the universe is expanding. The Hubble Space Telescope was named in his honor.

Scott Joplin (1868–1917) was born in Texas, but spent most of his life in Missouri. He was a piano player who helped develop a style of music called "ragtime." Joplin wrote such popular songs as "The Maple Leaf Rag" and "The Entertainer."

James Cash (J.C.) Penney (1875–1971) was born in Caldwell County. He started as a dry goods clerk and bought stock in a store named the Golden Rule Store. He bought more stores, which led to a nationwide chain called J.C. Penney.

Mary Lou Williams (1910–1981) was the First Lady of Jazz. She composed and arranged more music in any genre than any other person who has ever lived. She called Kansas City "a heavenly city" because of the number of jazz venues there.

For Jody Jensen Shaffer and Sue Lowell Gallion,
for seeing me through. —A.I.

For Jeff, my travel partner and co-pilot in
life's adventures. —L.H.B.

STERLING CHILDREN'S BOOKS
New York

An Imprint of Sterling Publishing Co., Inc.
1166 Avenue of the Americas
New York, NY 10036

Text © 2017 by Ann Ingalls
Illustrations © 2017 by Laura Huliska-Beith

ISBN 978-1-4549-2075-5
Distributed in Canada by Sterling Publishing
C/o Canadian Manda Group, 664 Annette Street
Toronto, Ontario, Canada M6S 2C8
Distributed in the United Kingdom by GMC Distribution Services
Castle Place, 166 High Street, Lewes, East Sussex, England BN7 1XU
Distrubuted in Australia by NewSouth Books, 45 Coogee, NSW 2034, Australia

For information about custom editions, special sales, and premium and
corporate purchases, please contact Sterling Special Sales at
800-805-5489 or specialsales@sterlingpublishing.com.

Manufactured in China
Lot #:
2 4 6 8 10 9 7 5 3 1
07/17

www.sterlingpublishing.com

Design by Sharon Jacobs

The original illustrations for this book were created by hand using acrylic paint, then collaged digitally in Photoshop.

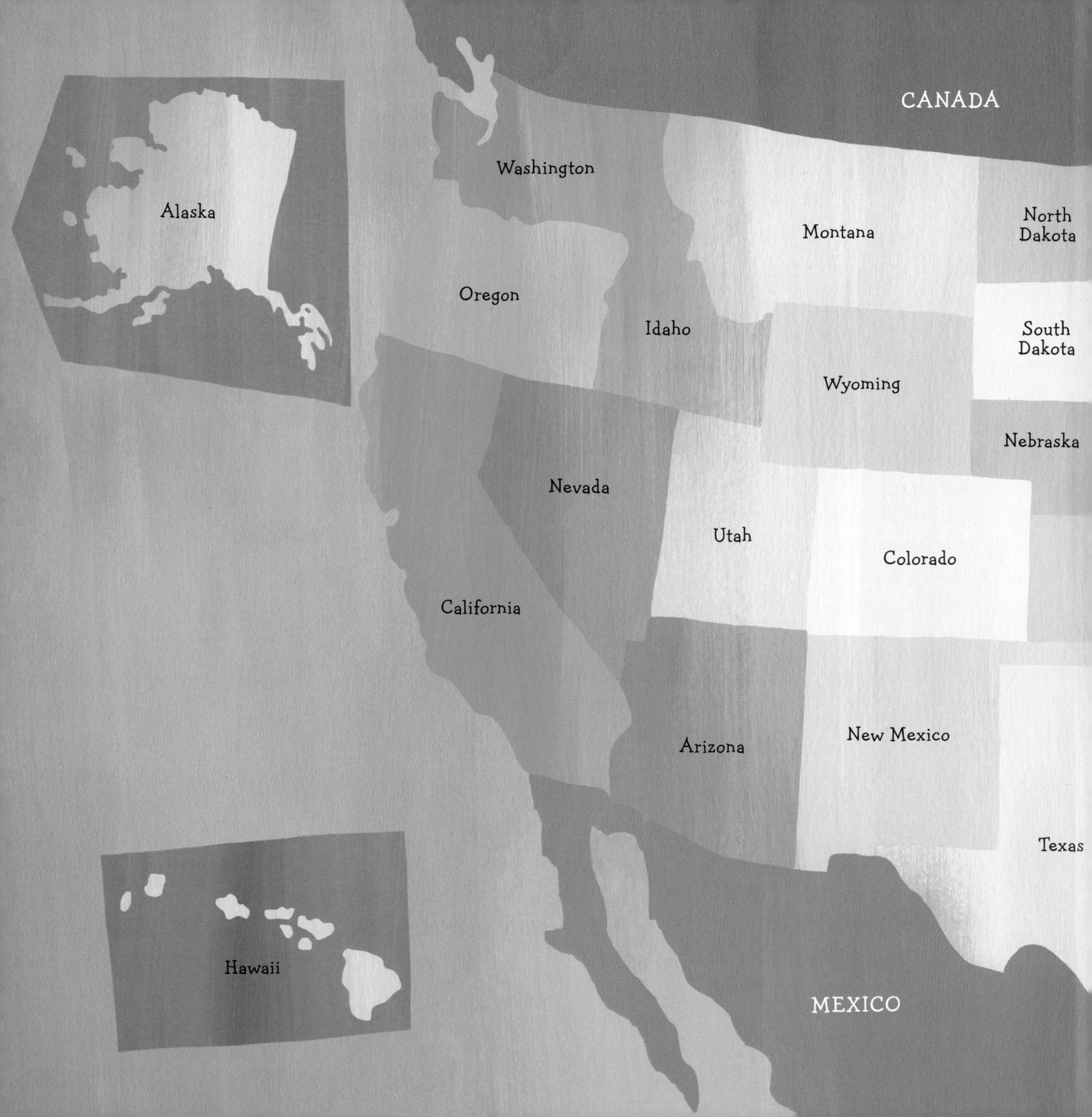

CANADA

Alaska

Washington

Montana

North
Dakota

Oregon

Idaho

South
Dakota

Wyoming

Nevada

Nebraska

Utah

Colorado

California

Arizona

New Mexico

Texas

Hawaii

MEXICO